Playing with
Bart learns a hard lesson about fire danger

Digital Book · Print Book · Activity book · Audio Book · Read-Along Video

This Book Bundle Includes 5 Additional Versions
Please visit our website for purchasing details
http://kiddy-books.biz/Bart

Sylvia Yordanova

Website: *http://kiddy-books.biz*
Printed in the United States of America
First Printing, 2016
ISBN-13: 978-1539344643
ISBN-10: 1539344649

CROWDFUNDING with INDIEGOGO

https://igg.me/at/fireDanger

Dear Parents,

This book bundle **Playing with Fire** is involved in Indiegogo crowd funding project. We are determined to distribute it in as many nurseries, schools and libraries as possible. We are working with many fire departments, who are excited to work with us and distribute the book bundle. This will help fire departments spread the word about fire safety within schools and communities.

Some responses we already had from USA Fire Districts:

"Bravo! What a valuable and worthwhile venture on behalf of our children. We will post the names of the book/video and link to the book on the fire department website on the Fire Safety page. I would also ask you reach out the local Public School district."

"We have a comprehensive fire prevention program with our local schools which we visit every year and we would be happy to include this in our education program. Also, we will be interested in purchasing the book to hand out to students."

On our page, https://igg.me/at/fireDanger you can find many perks for our sponsors. Please, support us and let us help kids and their families to be safe and happy. With your donation (starting from $ 1), we can make this book fun and educational. Beyond money- we need your help spreading the word. We'd be eternally grateful if you would share the crowd funding link and information with your friends, family, neighbours, educators, co-workers, librarians, and everyone about this book! Thank you!

Hello! My name is Bart. I like going out with my friends. We have a lot of fun.

Here are my friends. They are Charlie the dog, Oberon the tortoise and Bella the rabbit. One day we decided to go for a walk in the nearby forest. We walked for a long time and became very hungry. So we stopped for something to eat.

 I wanted a hot dog, so I started a fire and threw the
match into the bushes.

"Hey, Bart" yelled Charlie, "You should never do
that!"

"Do what?" I was confused.

"Throw a lit match into the forest." Charlie was
furious.

"Stop worrying Charlie." I said, "The match was
almost out."

"One small spark could set the whole forest on fire."
"I already said it was almost out. What is wrong with
you?" I was getting annoyed.

"What Charlie is saying is true Bart," Bella chimed in,
"You need to be more careful."
"OK, but I don't understand why you both are so upset
over such a little thing."
"It's not a little thing!" Bella exclaimed. "And put out
that fire when you are finished cooking." She added as
she started walking away with Charlie and Oberon.

"Alright, alright," I said, shaking my head. I poured some water on the fire and stomped it with my feet, making sure it was completely out. Then I hurried to catch up with my friends.

When I finally caught up with them, I could see they
were still angry.
"You have to learn to think before you act Bart."
Charlie was the first to speak. "Do you know what a
fire would do to the forest?" He asked.

I kept silent as Charlie continued. "It would kill many animals, birds, and insects."
"And tortoises like me who can't move very fast," Oberon said.
"And rabbits like me can get trapped in their burrows. Bella said.

"Let's keep going, guys. I think Bart understands and won't be careless with fire again." Charlie said as he started walking away.

I was getting tired of my friends picking on me and telling me what to do.
"OK, since you guys are so smart you can go on without me!" I said in a huff.

"We aren't saying you're stupid Bart. We just want you to understand how dangerous fire can be." Bella stated in a soothing voice.
"You guys make it sound like that. I see the adults light fires all the time. Never mind." I started walking away.

"Don't go, Bart," Oberon called out.
I was hurt and angry. I kept walking away.

I went away by myself. I stopped for a swim in the river and found a bee hive in a tree. The honey made a delicious snack, but I was still hungry.

In my pack, I found some marshmallows. I made another fire and roasted them. My friends didn't know what they were missing!

I lay down for a nap. My tummy was full, and I needed to rest. I went to sleep by the tree without properly putting out the fire.

I awoke to the smell of smoke and watched in horror as the blaze quickly spread.

My eyes were stinging, and I
could barely breathe.
The smoke was everywhere!

Through the smoke, I could see that the flames were all around me. It reached for my clothes and shoes. I was scared! I moved quickly away from it.

 The little fire I made had grown to a big one, and I
didn't know what to do.
I was scared. "Help! Help! Help! Somebody, please
help me!" I cried out.

I overheard the animals screaming as they ran away.
Then I heard the voices of my friends.

Would they come to help, after I treated them so badly?
"Help me! Help me!" I continued to scream.
I ran to my friends as fast as I could.

My friends heard me and came to help. With a
blanket from their pack and water from the river, they
quickly put the fire out.
Thankfully, it was not such a big fire and it was soon
over.

I was scared and not feeling well. The heat and smoke made me cough and choke. My friends helped me walk because I was so weak.

Oberon stomped out the last of the flames. Making
sure the fire was completely out.

"I'm sorry I didn't listen to you." My friends gathered around as I continued, "I started a fire to roast some marshmallows, but forgot to put it out when I went to sleep." I was ashamed.

"Bart, how could you, after what we already told you?" Bella asked.

"It's alright. The fire wasn't so big, and I think that Bart learned a valuable lesson today." Charlie said.

"Yes, I did. Fire is very serious and shouldn't be used so carelessly."

Boys and girls, I was very lucky my friends came to help. But all of that could have been avoided if I would have listened to them about the dangers of playing with fire. I will never play with fire again.

Please write to me and tell my friends and me what you would do if a fire starts at home or school.
It's important that we all know about fire safety and have a plan.

Ask your Mom and Dad about making a safety plan in case of a fire, or any other emergency. Write it down and send it to me and my friends so we know what to do. Paint, or draw us a picture with your letter so you can help teach Charlie, Bella, Oberon and me what to do.

We will post your letters and drawings to our website: www.kiddy-books.biz/Bart

As a thank you, we will send you another one of our stories.

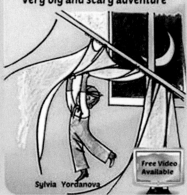

35

60 pages
Supplementary
Activity Book for Kids Ages 4-8

Digital Book   Print Book   Activity Book   Audio Book   YouTube Read-Along

www.kiddy-books.biz/Bart

Made in the USA
Middletown, DE
01 August 2017